# Waiting for Mr. Goose

WRITTEN BY **Laurie Lears**

ILLUSTRATED BY **Karen Ritz**

Albert Whitman & Company

Morton Grove, Illinois

To Jeff, my husband and best friend.

And with thanks to Amanda, whose compassion

and patience saved Zack the goose. — L. L.

For Tommy and his family. — K. R.

Library of Congress Cataloging-in-Publication Data

Lears, Laurie.
Waiting for Mr. Goose / by Laurie Lears ; illustrated by Karen Ritz.
p.  cm.
Summary: Stephen, who has trouble sitting still and paying attention,
surprises himself when he summons up the patience to catch
and help an injured goose. Includes a note to adults about children
who have difficulty staying focused, including those with ADHD.
ISBN 0-8075-8628-5
[1. Attention-deficit hyperactivity disorder — Fiction.
2. Geese — Fiction.   3. Wildlife rescue — Fiction.]
I. Ritz, Karen, ill. II. Title.
PZ7.L46365Wai  1999
[E]—dc21   99-10698   CIP

Text copyright © 1999 by Laurie Lears.
Illustrations copyright © 1999 by Karen Ritz.
Published in 1999 by Albert Whitman & Company,
6340 Oakton Street, Morton Grove, Illinois 60053-2723.
Published simultaneously in Canada by General Publishing, Limited, Toronto.
Printed in the United States of America.
10 9 8 7 6 5 4 3 2 1

The illustrations were done in watercolor on fabreano paper.
The design is by Scott Piehl.

# Note

Waiting is difficult for all children. With their boundless energy and limited perception of time, young children can only gradually develop patience.

Those who have AD/HD contend with greater obstacles in their quest for self-control. They struggle to sustain concentration and attentiveness while their minds and bodies race ahead in high gear. For each step forward, they may fall two steps back.

Although children with AD/HD often grow accustomed to negative feedback from others, I've seen assets associated with this disorder. These children tend to be innovative, creative thinkers, and once their energy is channeled, they possess a tenacity that is unstoppable.

It is important that all children recognize their strengths and experience success as they navigate their way towards maturity.

— Laurie Lears

Stephen was always on the go. At breakfast he sloshed juice onto the table. "Slow down!" his mom said.

On the school bus he bounced and squirmed in his seat. "Sit still!" said the driver.

At school he tapped his pencils against the desk and missed the teacher's directions. "Pay attention!" said Mr. Timmons.

Stephen felt as if he couldn't do anything right.

After school he set off for the pond near his house. He ran along the banks, skipped stones across the water, and swung from the trees. And no one told him to slow down, sit still, or pay attention.

He watched the geese on the other side of the pond and wished he could be wild and free like them.

One day he noticed a goose that was limping. Stephen peered closely. Clamped on the goose's leg was a small metal trap with a chain dangling from it. Stephen dashed home to get help.

His mom called the nature center, and a man named Mr. Frye came to catch the goose. Stephen tried to steer the goose in Mr. Frye's direction, but the goose flew off towards the meadow.

Mr. Frye shook his head. "As long as he can fly, we won't catch him," he said, "though Mr. Goose will be in real trouble if that chain gets hooked on something."

"Let's keep trying!" Stephen begged. But Mr. Frye was already on his way back to his truck.

That night Stephen tossed and turned in bed. He gazed through his window into the inky darkness and worried about Mr. Goose.

Stephen was up early the next day. He found an old net in the garage and dragged it to the pond. There were four geese huddled near the water. "I hope one of you is Mr. Goose," Stephen whispered. And sure enough, when he came closer, he saw the trap on one goose's leg.

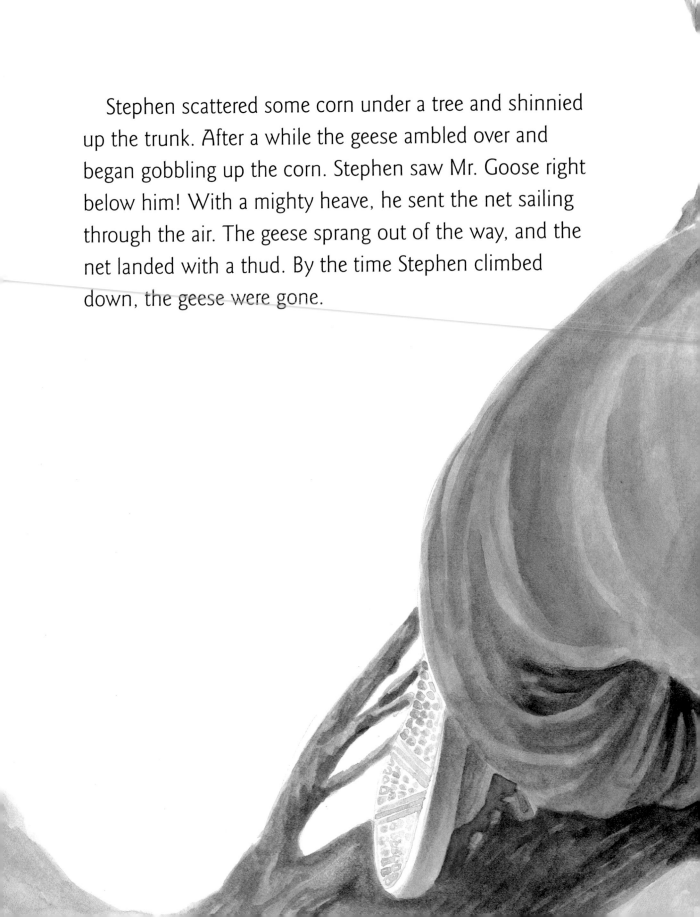

Stephen scattered some corn under a tree and shinnied up the trunk. After a while the geese ambled over and began gobbling up the corn. Stephen saw Mr. Goose right below him! With a mighty heave, he sent the net sailing through the air. The geese sprang out of the way, and the net landed with a thud. By the time Stephen climbed down, the geese were gone.

The next morning Stephen crept to the pond with Dad's big work gloves on his hands. This time he would catch Mr. Goose for sure!

He barely breathed as he crawled towards the geese. But all at once, they saw him coming and flapped noisily away. Stephen raced behind them. He plunged through prickly weeds, leaped over logs, and clambered up a rocky hill.

"Stupid goose!" he shouted. "I'm just trying to help you!"

When he reached the top of the hill, the geese were out of sight.

Suddenly Stephen realized how frightened Mr. Goose must be. He was never going to catch him by tricking or chasing him.

Stephen walked home, thinking of another way to help Mr. Goose.

"I'll put corn at the pond every day and wait until Mr. Goose gets used to me," he told his parents.

"That sounds like a good idea!" said Mom.

Stephen frowned. "But I'm not so good at waiting," he said.

"It's worth a try," said Dad. "Maybe you'll surprise yourself."

From then on Stephen walked quietly to the pond. He emptied a bag of corn in the same place each day and stood far away to wait. Finally the geese came to eat, but they kept their eyes on Stephen.

Little by little, he was able to get closer to the geese. Stephen's body felt wiggly, though. He longed to skip stones across the water or swing from the willow tree. But he knew the geese were just beginning to trust him.

One afternoon he sprinkled the corn into a pile and took only two steps back. His breath came out in steamy puffs, and his hands and feet grew heavy with cold. He had to shut his eyes and bite his lip to keep from moving.

Stephen felt something stirring around his feet. He opened his eyes. There was Mr. Goose, pecking right next to his shoe! Stephen slowly lifted his foot and stepped firmly on the chain hanging from the trap. His heart thumped in his ears as he took off his jacket and slipped it over Mr. Goose. Mr. Goose gave a startled honk, but he did not try to get away.

Stephen sank to the ground, holding the heavy bundle close. He rocked back and forth to stay warm and sang a song to Mr. Goose. "It was sure hard to wait . . . And now it is late . . . But soon you'll be free, Mr. Goose!"

The sky turned the color of smoke. And at last Stephen saw his mom hurrying down the path.

"Stephen!" she called. But suddenly she stopped and put her hand over her mouth. "You caught him!" she whispered.

Stephen nodded and tears stung his eyes. He could hardly believe he was holding Mr. Goose.

His mom gently pried the trap from Mr. Goose's leg, and Stephen removed his jacket. Mr. Goose stumbled to his feet, blinking his eyes. He beat his wings and rose into the air. But before disappearing into the dusky sky, he flew in a circle around the pond.

"Look, Stephen!" cried his mom. "I think he's saying thank you!"

Stephen grinned and waved. "You're welcome, Mr. Goose!" he called.

Then Stephen turned four cartwheels
in a row before heading back home with
his mom.